The MacDougall Twins With Sherlock Holmes

Book #1: The Amazing Airship Adventure

Paperback ISBN 9781780927107
ePub ISBN 9781780927114
PDF ISBN 9781780927121

Published in the UK by MX Publishing
335 Princess Park Manor, Royal Drive, London, N11 3GX
www.mxpublishing.co.uk

Cover Illustration by Brian Belanger
Cover Compilation by www.staunch.com

Dedication

For Rhea -

My dear friend, harsh critic, and loving daughter

Table of Contents

London, 1897

Chapter 1: Dinner with Sherlock Holmes

Sherlock Holmes heard a loud, "knock, knock, knock," at the door of his home. With a smile, the great detective rose from his favorite easy chair, and went to personally greet his visitors. "Mrs. Hudson and Dr. Watson," Sherlock called to his landlady and his good friend, "do be so kind as to let me answer the door."

Mrs. Hudson was working very hard in the kitchen, making sure the potatoes were not overly done. Dr. Watson was checking on the goose they were having for dinner. Mrs. Hudson gave Sherlock a quick nod of her head in approval, and then she went back to checking on the gravy.

Sherlock Holmes had special guests tonight, two of the best detectives he had ever worked with. These two twins, Jimmy and Emma MacDougall, had helped Sherlock Holmes send the art thief Byron Von Trapp to prison. It did not matter to Mr. Holmes that the twins were only ten years old. They were honest, brilliant, and brave.

Sherlock opened the door and greeted his friends warmly. "Hello, hello, please do come in," he said to everyone.

The family was standing at the entryway. Mr. MacDougall felt very uncomfortable because he was wearing his best evening dress. He was a head chimney sweeper, and he preferred being in dirty clothes rather than dressing up for a dinner party. As he walked in, he said, "Hello, Mr. Holmes. Very gracious of you inviting us over like this."

"Nedley," Sherlock said to him, "It is my pleasure. I see you were working on State Street today."

Mr. MacDougall looked surprised. "Why Mr. Holmes, how do you know? I washed up proper."

"Of course you did," Sherlock said. "Still, the color of the ash on your thumb, mixed with the smell of soot in your hair, leads me to only one conclusion about your work location."

"And Frances," he said to Mrs. MacDougall. "I see you were working on a new quilt today."

Mrs. MacDougall smiled and entered the house in her flowing gray dress. "That's right, Mr. Holmes." Mrs. MacDougall didn't want to hear about how Sherlock Holmes knew about her sewing. She did not like that her children were friends with the detective. They were always getting into trouble, and she was afraid one day they would get hurt.

Next came the guests of honor. Sherlock stared at the two twins. Jimmy and Emma were not identical twins, but they looked remarkably similar. Both had freckled faces, smooth fiery red hair, and sparkling blue eyes. They were both tall for their ages. Jimmy stood at five and a half feet tall, and Emma's height was just over five feet. Both wore dark clothing, Jimmy in a black suit and Emma in a long sleeved dress.

"I see you have been practicing the violin today, Mr. Holmes," Emma said, showing Holmes that she also could use the power of deduction.

Sherlock grinned. "Is it because of the way I am holding my left arm?"

"Naw," Jimmy added, "It's because we could hear you playing all afternoon."

Sherlock laughed. Emma had the brains and skill to be just as good a detective as Mr. Holmes. Jimmy was the joker, and while he was good at using deduction to solve crimes, he preferred going undercover to catch a thief.

Suddenly, they all heard a shout of, "Don't stand there at the door. Dinner is served."

"We must not keep Mrs. Hudson waiting," Emma said, and the three entered the home.

"I guess this will be a bit of a boring night," Jimmy said to Sherlock. "No cases today."

Sherlock laughed. "One never knows when a case might turn up." Little did Mr. Holmes know that a case was just about to begin.

Chapter 2: The Flying Barrel

Everyone sat down at dinner and served themselves by passing the plates. As Dr. Watson scooped potatoes and cut himself a piece of goose breast, he asked the twins, "Jimmy, Emma, how is your detective work going these days?"

"Dr. Watson," Mrs. MacDougall snapped at him, "must we talk about their cases at the dinner table? You know how I feel about them telling you about their adventures. I don't want you writing down their stories."

Dr. Watson was known for publishing stories about Sherlock Holmes's most famous cases. He always wanted to write down the mysteries that the MacDougall twins solved, but Mrs. MacDougall refused to let him. She did not want her children to be famous. She wanted them to have a normal life.

"You can't blame me for trying," Dr. Watson laughed, and he winked at the twins. He knew they wanted to tell their stories, but they respected their mother's wishes.

"You still should bring the twins to my office next week," Watson continued, changing the subject. "I haven't checked up on them in nearly six months."

"Oh, the kids are fine, Dr. Watson," Mr. MacDougall explained. "Not even a skinned knee on Jimmy."

"It is still wise to have them looked after by a doctor," Sherlock Holmes said. "Sometimes small problems you don't see turn out to be big problems later. This reminds me of the case of the Man with the Missing Right Hand."

"They look fine to me," Mrs. Hudson chimed in, interrupting the detective. She did not want to hear yet another retelling of a famous case.

"I can't get over how much the twins have grown," Mrs. Hudson said to their parents. "I've watched them turn from babies into a fine young man and woman." Mr. and Mrs. MacDougall grinned at the compliment.

"Thank you, Mrs. Hudson. Now, no more talk of detective work," Mrs. MacDougall firmly stated, glaring directly at Holmes and Watson. "Let's enjoy this fine dinner and talk about happy topics, no robbers tonight please."

Everyone nodded in agreement, although Jimmy frowned, wishing the conversation would be about robbers and crime. *What is the point of eating dinner with Sherlock Holmes,* he wondered, *if I can't talk to him about mysteries?*

The dinner conversation continued pleasantly until...

"AAAHH!" came screams from the street.

"What is it?" someone else yelled. Sherlock Holmes dashed to the window. Everyone followed him. They all crowded around, looking out at the skyline.

"Emma, are you seeing what I'm seeing?" Jimmy asked his sister.

"Yes, Jimmy, I...I see it too."

Floating above London was a strange, giant object. To Jimmy it looked like a giant flying silver barrel. It was the size of two busses put together, with great curved wings on its side, almost like someone put the barrel in the middle of an enormous boomerang. The flying object seemed to come straight out of space. It was slowly gliding over the buildings, causing shouts and cries from the streets of London below. Suddenly, the aircraft turned in the sky

and swiftly swooped towards Baker Street.

"Goodness, Holmes," Dr. Watson said. "It is heading straight for the street below."

The detective motioned with his hand for his friend to stay quiet. He was observing everything, and he didn't want to miss any details.

A giant crowd had gathered in Baker Street as the aircraft floated towards them. Some **hansom cabs**[1], a **bus**, and several people on horses stopped and joined the growing crowd, gazing up at the object. Some pointed, others talked. A few people fled as the object came towards them, blocking out the sun. Suddenly, the shiny silver barrel stopped right above the crowd. It hovered for a mere moment, then FLASH! A huge blinding light shot out from the bottom of the craft. Everyone screamed and scattered. The horses neighed and screeched, then bolted in opposite directions. Two **hansom cabs** flipped over as their horses bolted away from the blinding light. The bus flung out of control right below Sherlock Holmes and the dinner guests. The

---

[1] **Fun Facts:** In the time period of this story, the automobile hadn't yet been invented. Everyone traveled by train, boat, or horse drawn carriage. A **hansom cab** was a two wheel carriage driven by a single horse. A **bus** (or omnibus) was a long carriage, driven by two horses, with seats along the sides.

The first image (below, left) shows a hansom cab, and the second an omnibus.

driver was able to regain control of the horses just as the bus almost crashed straight into 221 B Baker Street.

"Oh, those poor people," Mrs. O' Hare cried and turned away.

"At least they're safe," Mrs. Hudson consoled her.

"Look!" Jimmy called out. "The barrel...It's going to crash!"

The barrel ship began to quickly lower itself onto the street below. Just as its nose was about to smash into the ground, the ship wobbled, and then, seeming to defy gravity, it suddenly shot back up into the sky. It bobbed up and down slightly, and returned to its journey above Baker Street.

"Oh! It is going to fly right by us," Emma said excitedly.

As the ship flew up past the window, Emma got a good look at the device. Below the giant silver ship, there appeared to be a small cargo hold, with a man on what looked to be a pedal of sorts. The man seemed to be running and steering the mystery ship, as if it was a bicycle.

Just as Emma peered forward to get a better look, a blinding light flashed through the window. Everyone ducked down, moved away, and Mrs. Hudson shouted out in pain. No one could see anything. Suddenly, there was a sound of smashing glass, and something fell into the room.

Chapter 3: Ransom!

Mrs. Hudson, Dr. Watson, and the MacDougall parents called out in pain. Smoke and soot filled the air of the house, and shattered glass covered the floor. "Stay calm, everyone," the ten year old Emma reassured them. "It was the blinding flash of light from that aircraft. Your vision should return soon."

Sure enough, Dr. Watson started seeing the return of blurry shapes, and then, when his vision returned, he saw a startling sight. The apartment was a disaster. The dinner table was flipped on its side, and the food was splattered across the floor. Poor Mr. MacDougall was covered in gravy from his hair down to his belly. "What happened?" he called out.

"When I saw the light turning towards us, I did my best to shield everyone. Unfortunately, when I flipped up the table," Sherlock Holmes continued, "I only was able to shield the twins and myself."

"It's okay, Mr. Holmes," Mrs. MacDougall assured him while removing chunks of bread that had landed in her hair. "The children are top priority. Now, what happened to your beautiful window?"

Glass shards were sticking out of the carpet on the floor, and they were even embedded in the walls and ceiling. "This caused it, mom," explained Jimmy. He was holding up a large rock (more like a small boulder). Around the grey stone was tied a red ribbon, holding a rolled up paper. "It must have come from that thing in the sky."

"Good job, Jimmy," Sherlock said and grabbed the rock from the boy. He held it between his hands, lifted it towards the ceiling, and ran his finger through the grains of dirt still stuck to the rock's body. Then, he carefully slid the scroll out from the red ribbon, unrolled it, and read it over, his face turning grim.

"What's it say?" Mr. MacDougall asked.

Sherlock handed the letter over to Jimmy and Emma. "Take a look."

The letter was written in a strange format. It was made up of all capital letters cut from magazines and newspapers, and then glued together to form words. The note said,

MR. SHERLOCK HOLMES,

TELL YOUR BROTHER TO BRING ONE MILLION POUNDS TO 221 B BAKER STREET TOMORROW AT 5 OR ELSE ALL OF LONDON WILL SUFFER!

SINCERELY,

THE MAD BOMBER

"Oh, Heavens!" Mrs. Hudson called out. "You'd better tell Mycroft at once." Mycroft Holmes was the brother of Sherlock Holmes. He worked for the British government.

"Of course, Mrs. Hudson," Sherlock agreed, and he then added, "If you wouldn't mind, please wash up our guests, and find whatever food we have left in the icebox. We should still give the MacDougalls some dinner.

Even with all this excitement, I'm sure their bellies still need food."

"No need for that, Mr. Holmes," Mr. MacDougall started to say, but Mrs. Hudson stopped him.

"Now, now, Nedley. No guest of mine is going to go hungry, and we must feed the children," Mrs. Hudson assured him.

"Watson! We must be away at once." Sherlock and Dr. Watson grabbed their coats. Before leaving, Sherlock whispered to Emma and Jimmy, "Look out your window tonight. The light will be blinking."

"What are you whispering over there?" Mrs. MacDougall asked, making sure the twins were not getting into trouble.

"Just making sure they weren't hurt, Frances," Holmes explained to Mrs. MacDougall.

The twins nodded and didn't say anything. The light blinking meant only one thing - Sherlock Holmes needed their help!

+++

That night, after their parents were asleep, Jimmy went to Emma's bedroom. He gave a soft, "knock-knock," at his sister's door, so as not to wake their parents. His father's loud snoring echoed up the hallway.

"It took you long enough, Jimmy," Emma said. "Sherlock may contact us at any minute."

"I wanted to make sure mom and dad were asleep. When dad's snores shake the house, I know I have nothing to worry about." Jimmy and Emma laughed. Then Jimmy added, "I was going through my books on trains and coaches, and then, look what I found!"

Jimmy showed Emma a long thin book called <u>Balloon Flight</u>. Inside was a picture of what looked like the strange object they had seen in the sky that day.

"That thing is called an airship," Jimmy explained. "It's a kind of hot air balloon, but it is steerable. There are a few different types."

Jimmy turned the page, and Emma saw pictures of three different types of airships: one looked like a balloon, one like a hot dog in the sky, and the last one looked like the flying barrel they saw in the sky that day.

"See!" Jimmy said, excitedly pointing to the third picture. "That's a solid body airship. The frame is metal, surrounded by canvas, and it is huge. It could lift this house into the sky! I don't think we are dealing with a normal crook. I think we are dealing with a genius."

"I know," Emma agreed. "The mad bomber is very smart. He cut out those newspaper clippings, so we couldn't check his handwriting, and I believe he didn't leave any fingerprints either. I wish I could have taken a better look at that note."

"Well, Sherlock Holmes noticed something," Jimmy agreed. "I could see it in his face. If you had seen the note, I know you would have seen it too. I don't know how you two do it. Sherlock Holmes and you look at a piece of paper, and the two of you can figure out where it came from, and who wrote on it."

"You just have to pay attention, Jimmy. It isn't magic. You just need to look for clues and...Wait! There he is!" Emma called, dashing to her window. She saw the silhouette of Holmes across the way.

"What's he doing?" asked Jimmy.

Sherlock held the candle up to the window. Then, he covered the light with a hand. He kept doing this over and over again, sometimes quickly covering up the flame, and other times leaving it out longer.

"He's sending us a coded message," Emma said. "Jimmy?"

"Got it," he said, handing Emma her journal. She wrote down the message Mr. Holmes was sending them.

TWINS-

I NEED YOU TO CHECK WITH YOUR SOURCES. LONDON IS IN DANGER. FIND OUT EVERYTHING YOU CAN ABOUT THE AIRSHIP.

Jimmy knew just what Sherlock Holmes wanted them to do; they had to talk with the children of London, and find out what they knew about the airship. When Sherlock Holmes needed extra help, he often asked Jimmy and Emma to check with their friends. Many times, kids saw so much more than adults, who were so busy, that they did not pay attention to the world around them. Many adults probably did not even notice the airship in the sky. They were thinking about work, or bills, or some other nonsense.

Emma and Jimmy knew that Sherlock Holmes trusted them, and they had been given an important assignment. All of London, maybe even England, depended on their success.

Emma sent back a message to Sherlock Holmes.

DON'T WORRY MR. HOLMES. THE MACDOUGALL TWINS ARE ON THE CASE.

Chapter 4: Escaping School

"This is about Sherlock Holmes and that sky ship, ain't it?" Mr. MacDougall asked in a whisper while buttering his toast. He didn't want Mrs. MacDougall, who was in the next room hemming a dress, to hear them discussing a case.

Emma and Jimmy were asking their father for help. The twins needed to figure out a way to get out of their home that morning, and Mrs. MacDougall never let them leave school early, unless their dad had a task for them.

"Dad, you've got to help us," Emma begged.

"Mr. Holmes needs our help. All of London is in danger," added Jimmy. "Come on, Dad!"

"Okay, okay, if Mr. Holmes needs your help, then I'll send Laurence over to fetch you. But you'd better stay caught up on your school work," Mr. MacDougall sternly stated.

The twins promised, and Mr. MacDougall said goodbye, then headed out to clean the city chimneys.

Emma and Jimmy were schooled at home by their mother. Most of the children in London worked either in factories or in businesses, even if they were only five years old. Some went away to live at school. Mrs. MacDougall did not want her children working, and she did not want them away from home for a very long time. She taught the twins in their home in the morning, and she had them run errands for her in the afternoon.

This morning Jimmy was working on his math skills, called arithmetic, and Emma was learning about the history of the earth, when giant animals known as dinosaurs ruled the land. Most girls only learned how to sit up straight, sew, and have good manners. Mrs. MacDougall made sure that Emma had the same schooling as Jimmy. She thought it was a waste for girls to not have the same options as boys. In fact, Emma was even smarter than Jimmy.

Jimmy finished up his math booklet, and Emma paused to check his work. It gave the twins a chance to talk without their mother knowing they were investigating the airship mystery.

"You solved most of the problems correctly, but you made errors solving some fraction problems," Emma explained. "Do numbers four, five, and nine again."

Jimmy frowned and snatched his book back. "The only thing I need to solve is this airship mystery."

"Do you think Laurence will have heard from anyone?" asked Emma.

Laurence was a chimney sweep who worked with Mr. MacDougall. That morning, Jimmy had his dad give Laurence a message to send telegrams to the twins' friends. Messages were sent to Steve the steel worker, Sally the seamstress, Nolan the newspaper boy, and Thomas the tailor to see if they knew anything about the airship. Once the friends received the message, word would spread, and soon all the children in London would be looking for airship clues.

"I bet he did. I mean, that ship was the size of a flying herd of elephants. Everyone should have seen it."

Surprisingly, there was no news of the airship in the morning paper.

Just then, there came a knock on the door. "Now, who could that be?" Mrs. MacDougall said, while getting up from her sewing. Mrs. MacDougall was a seamstress who hemmed, mended, and made clothes for a job. She worked at home, so she could also teach Jimmy and Emma.

The twins heard their mother answer the door and have a brief conversation. "He needs them now! Really, Laurence, you tell Nedley not to bother the children until afternoon, after their school work is completed." There was another brief talk, and then Mrs. MacDougall said, "All right! All right! They can go now!"

Mrs. MacDougall called to the twins to come to the door. "Children, your father needs your help this morning. One of his chimney sweeps is sick, and Emma, he needs your help understanding a bill he has received. Both of you will go with Laurence, but Laurence will make sure you return as soon as you can. You will need to make up all of your missed time from school this afternoon. The sooner you return, the better. School is too important to miss. You will finish your lessons today, even if you finish at midnight."

"Yes Mom," the twins agreed. Laurence thanked Mrs. MacDougall, and the three were off into the city streets.

Laurence was huffing and puffing a bit as they walked together. He was a plump old man, who Emma would have said looked a bit like Father Christmas, except he was covered in black soot from head to toe. He left a strange trail of dark footprints behind him as he waddled along.

"You can slow down a bit," Jimmy assured Laurence, who was wheezing from running to the MacDougall house. "Any responses to our telegrams?"

"Just one," Laurence wheezed. "From...(huff)... Nolan." Laurence caught his breath, and he wiped the sweat from his brow. The chimney sweep then continued. "There doesn't seem to be much news about a flying boat, or what have you. Now, I've got to dash back to work. Your dad wanted me to tell you to stay out of trouble. No sense in that though. If you're chasing flying boats, I know you'll get up to some kind of mischief."

"It's an airship," Emma explained. "It scared a whole crowd of people. I don't know why no one is talking about it!"

"Baah!" Laurence said, with a dismissing wave of his arm. "Next you'll be seeing the Ghost of Christmas Past. Oh! Look at the time!" Laurence added, looking at his pocket watch. "I have to get back to work!" He said goodbye and ran down the street as fast as he could. Jimmy thought, from behind, he looked like a penguin scampering away.

"Just Nolan," Emma said. "Only Nolan has news. That's strange. That ship caused quite a stir on Baker Street. More of London must have seen it. Why didn't anyone else report anything? Why just Nolan?"

"Well, Nolan is the newspaper boy," Jimmy joked. "He should have news for us."

Chapter 5: Nolan and the Mysterious Stranger

Jimmy and Emma raced along Baker Street as fast as their legs could carry them. They had to get to Nolan, to find out what he knew of the airship and the Mad Bomber.

"Slow down a little, Jimmy," Emma called after her brother. She was having a hard time keeping up with him, as they zig-zagged along the sidewalk.

"I can't!" he called back. "I don't want Mom making me do school work until midnight! Anyway, we're here."

The youth stopped at a bustling intersection full of traffic. It was the entrance to the London Underground Railway. Horse drawn carriages lined the road, waiting to pick up passengers. Business men in suits and ties walked about in a hurry. Some of them headed down, underground, to catch a train, and others came up from a train that had arrived. Standing at the entrance to the Baker Street

Underground Station was Nolan - a young, grimy looking boy, standing on a wooden crate and yelling "Extra! Extra! Read all about it! King and Queen of Spain to visit London!"

The twins approached Nolan the newsboy; his greasy blond hair stuck out at odd angles, and his shirt and pants had multiple patches to hold them together. A gentleman approached the boy, gave him a few pence, and took a copy of the paper.

"Thank you, sir," Nolan said, and then he turned and saw Jimmy and Emma. "Hey, it's the MacDougall twins. Boy, have I got news for you."

"You have news about the airship?" Emma asked.

"Sure, sure," Nolan continued. "I got to make this fast though. These papers don't sell themselves," Nolan added, pointing to a stack of fifty newspapers at his feet.

Jimmy reached into his pocket and handed Nolan over a few pence. "Thank you, muchly," Nolan said, pocketing the coins and handing Jimmy a copy of the *Times*.

"Anyway, so I was meeting some of the boys yesterday, in front of the office of the *Daily Times Gazette,* because Henry, one of us newsboys, had come down with a bad cold. He was so sick, he couldn't sell his papers. We, the boys and I, were meeting to divide up his papers and add them to our piles. If someone's out sick, we sell their papers for them, so they don't lose their money for the day. You can't eat if you don't have food, I always say."

"What does this have to do with the mad bomber?" Jimmy asked. He was getting nervous. They only had six hours left to solve the case before the mad bomber would strike again.

"I'm getting to that. Let me tell the story," Nolan said. "Anyway, as we are standing out front, this strange man kicks open the door of the newspaper office and storms out. He yells back, 'I'll show you a real story! You'll see just how real my story is tonight!' And, he starts to march away. Then, he sees me and the boys, and comes straight at us. I thought he was gonna yell at us, too. Instead, he comes right up to me and says, 'You there! Give me one of those papers!'

"He snatches one out of my hand, looks at the headline, and says 'Bah! You think this is news. Just wait till tomorrow, then all of London will know real news!' Then, he wandered off into a cab and took off down the street."

"Did you get a good look at him?" Emma asked. She thought this sounded just like the mad bomber.

"Course I did," Nolan said proudly. "But the guy was real funny looking, like he didn't want anyone to know who he was. He wore a long, black overcoat, **pince-nez glasses**[2], but with the lens darkened, so I couldn't make out his eye color...Oh yes! And a deerstalker hat, with the flaps down, to cover his ears."

"That doesn't tell us too much," Jimmy said.

"Let me finish," Nolan went on. "He had a sharp nose, well-trimmed dark beard and mustache, and the coach he went off in, it had initials on the side. In big writing were the letters S.H.

"S.H.!" the twins shouted together.

"That's what I said, and that's what I meant," Nolan concluded, and he leaped back on

---

[2] **Fun Fact:** Pince-nez glasses are small, foldable glasses that were popular in the 19th century. Unlike modern glasses, pince-nez glasses had no stems to rest on ears. They were held in place by a spring that grips or "pinches" the nose.

The images show two different styles of pince-nez glasses.

top of his crate. "Anyway, I got to get back to work. Hope that helps you and all."

"One last thing, Nolan," Jimmy added. "Who was the stranger yelling at, in the newspaper office? We need to ask that man some questions."

"Good luck with that," Jimmy stated. "That was Old Man Withers, the news editor. He doesn't speak to anyone who doesn't have a story, and even if you did, he doesn't ever talk to children. In fact, he hates kids!"

"That's okay, Nolan. Thank you for the information," Emma said.

As she and Jimmy walked away, they heard Nolan begin calling out, "Extra! Extra!" again, and selling his papers.

"What do you think?" Jimmy asked his sister.

"It's not much," Emma conceded, "but it is a start. I think we need to split up. Jimmy, you need to talk with Old Man Withers and find out what the mad bomber said to him. Also, we need to know why he didn't print a story about the airship. Why was the story left out of all the papers?"

"Got it," Jimmy agreed.

"And I'll go see if I can find our friend Steven the cab driver. We need to find that cab with the initials S.H. on its side. That might be the clue to solving this case."

"I agree, but I'm a little worried about those letters and the deerstalker hat."

Emma frowned and nodded. They were both worried...but it couldn't be true, could it? With the deerstalker hat and the initials S.H...Could the mad bomber be...**Sherlock Holmes!**

Chapter 6: Jimmy in Disguise

Jimmy looked up at the towering building before him. *Will this work?* he wondered. *Do I look like an adult? What if Old Man Withers sees through my disguise?*

It had taken Jimmy a good hour to prepare, and he straightened his neck tie, adjusted his **monocle**[3], and made sure his top hat wouldn't fall off his head. With the help of makeup, and his spare dress up kit that was kept hidden with Sally the seamstress, Jimmy had transformed himself from a child to a full adult. Emma had always called Jimmy the

---

[3] **Fun Fact:** A monocle (pronounced mon-i-kull) is an eyeglass for one eye that is held up by the muscles around the eye.

The images below show two different styles of monocles, and a man wearing a monocle.

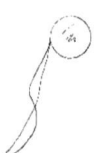 

master of disguise, and this was the part of detective work Jimmy loved best. In the past, Jimmy had gone undercover as a circus clown, a street performer, and even once as a blind Frenchman. Every time, he had successfully fooled people; one time, he'd even tricked his mother into thinking he was a young beggar, and she put a penny in his cup when he knocked at their door.

Now, as he entered the office of the *Daily Times Gazette* and approached the desk of Mr. Withers, he wondered if Old Man Withers would be the first person to see through one of his disguises. Nolan had said Mr. Withers hated kids. What if he could hear something in Jimmy's voice or see a piece of the costume that wasn't perfect? What if he yelled and chased Jimmy out onto the street? Jimmy shuddered as he found himself standing in front of Mr. Withers's desk.

"Excuse me, but are you Mr. Withers?" Jimmy asked the elderly white haired man, who was editing a news story.

Mr. Withers adjusted his spectacles, crossed out a few words on the paper before him, and then responded in a gruff voice, without looking up, "I am, and I am busy at the moment."

"But, I have a story I believe will be of interest to you. One that so many people will read, it could sell a million newspapers!" Jimmy said in as deep a voice as he could manage.

Mr. Withers looked up at the person before him and frowned. *Oh no!* Jimmy thought. *He sees through my disguise!* But instead of tossing Jimmy out onto the street, the old man gave a grin, revealing a mouth with many missing teeth.

It was not a boy that Mr. Withers saw before him, but a London gentleman. Jimmy was wearing a top hat and an overcoat. A fake mustache was glued below his nose, and a monocle was held in his right eye. Jimmy looked like a millionaire.

"Now, what story would that be?" asked Mr. Withers kindly.

Jimmy paused for a moment. Then, he realized his disguise had worked. He said to Mr. Withers, "Why, yesterday I saw a most extraordinary sight. There was a giant barrel shaped object that..."

"BAH!! Not another one!" Mr. Withers snapped at Jimmy. "You fell for that airship hoax."

"Hoax?" Jimmy asked surprised.

"Sure, it's a scam, a fake, people do them all the time. They create fake news stories, to try and trick the public and the newspapers. Another fellow told me the same story yesterday. He's probably the one who faked the whole thing. Trust me, it's nothing but a candle stick tied to a balloon in the sky. That's all you saw," Mr. Withers concluded, and then he turned back to editing the news. "Now, if you'll excuse me, I'm busy."

Jimmy couldn't believe it. The newspapers were not printing the story of the airship because no one thought it was real!

"You said another man brought you the story yesterday. Can you describe him for me? If he faked this airship, then I have some rough words for him!" Jimmy said, trying to sound tough.

"Not much to describe," Mr. Withers answered, and he gave the same description as Nolan, of the mysterious stranger. "Listen, don't let it upset you. These hoax stories come in all the time. You know, one time in America, they even printed a story about bat people living on the moon!"

Jimmy thanked Mr. Withers for his time. He left the news office feeling disappointed. He hadn't gotten any useful

information out of Mr. Withers. The twins now only had three hours to find the mad bomber and help Sherlock Holmes...unless Sherlock Holmes was the mad bomber. But how could Sherlock Holmes be the bomber? Jimmy and Emma were with him when the airship attacked. It was impossible, yet Sherlock Holmes could often perform the impossible. But if Sherlock Holmes was behind it all, then this must be some kind of test for Jimmy and

Emma. Sherlock Holmes would never hurt anyone. Was this a test? Jimmy found himself with many questions and no answers.

Just as Jimmy made it to the street in front of the newspaper office, a hansom cab pulled up in front of him. It was Steven the cab driver with Emma. She quickly opened the door to the carriage. "Get in!" she called out to Jimmy.

"What's the hurry?" Jimmy asked, as Emma yanked him into the cab, and Steven made the cab jolt into the busy London streets.

"Look!" Emma called and pointed ahead of them. Quickly moving along the street in front of them was a reddish colored wagon, pulled along by two galloping horses.

As the carriage barreled around a corner, Jimmy made out two distinct letters on its side...**S.H!**

Chapter 7: Chasing the Bomber

Steven the cab driver cracked his whip, and he made his horse gallop as fast as she could go. Jimmy and Emma felt like the cab they were in might fly off the road, at the speed Steven was going.

"Don't lose them, Steven," Emma called.

"I'm doing the best I can, miss, but he's got a four wheeler pulled by two cob horses. I've only got my Bess here, and she's going as fast as she can!" Steven called back. "Don't worry, ma'am, I won't lose him."

"Yeah, but I might lose my lunch," Jimmy said, while holding his belly. He wasn't used to fast motion and was feeling a little sick.

The two horse-drawn carriages continued to fly through London, past cathedrals and towers, swerving between bus carriages and people walking along the street. As they traveled, the mad bomber continued to get further and further away. Finally, they moved away from the busy streets of London and out into the countryside. Tree branches smashed against the side of the cab, and Bess gave an occasional loud, "Neigh!" But she didn't let up. The four wheeler in front of them remained in sight. They swerved along a forgotten, muddy road, and then suddenly, they could see a massive, pointed structure in front of them.

"What is that?" Emma asked.

"I know exactly what it is," said Jimmy. "It's a big top tent."

Steven brought the carriage to a halt with a loud "Whoa!" He made sure they weren't close to the tent, so no one in the tent would see them. The twins watched the four wheeled carriage, with S.H. on its side, stop right in front of the circus tent. Two big, gruff men got out, opened the doorway flaps, and the carriage disappeared into the tent.

"You did it, Steven!" Emma called out. She climbed out of the cab and gave the thin driver a big hug.

"Now, Miss," Steve said, turning a little red, "none of that mushy stuff. I owe you two kids for helping me dad out when he was in a jam, and no one else would believe he was innocent. You need something, you just ask me, okay?"

"I do have one more favor," Emma continued. "I need you to go back to town and tell Sherlock Holmes what we've discovered. Tell him about the chase, the tent, everything, and bring him back here."

"Of course, miss I...Wait a minute," Steven said, "What are you two up to? I can't leave you here all alone."

"We're just going to keep watch," Jimmy said, looking up at the 18 year old driver.

Steven's green eyes twinkled, and he gave a nod. "All right! If I know I can trust anyone, it's you two." With that, Steven called out to Bess, and the cab flew off back to London.

The twins watched the cab take off and waved goodbye to their trusted friend. Then, Jimmy said to Emma, "Come on, let's go see what's in that circus tent."

Emma laughed, "But, I thought you said we were just going to keep watch."

"Of course we are," Jimmy grinned. "We'll keep watch as we walk into that tent. And we'll keep watch as we discover just who that mad bomber is."

As the twins crept through the woods to the circus tent, they updated each other on what had happened when they were separated. Jimmy told Emma about the news office. In fact, he was still dressed in his outfit.

Emma told Jimmy how they found the mad bomber's carriage.

"I found Steven, and we started combing the streets of London, looking for that cab. As fortune would have it, we discovered his cab parked in front of an apothecary. Just as I was about to get out and investigate, the mad bomber got back into his carriage, and took off into the streets. Steven was able to follow him, and when he turned past the news office, we stopped to get you."

"Why would he need medicine?" Jimmy wondered.

"Let's find out," Emma said. They had made their way to the circus tent. It was tied down in many spots, but the twins lifted a flap and were able to sneak in.

What they discovered amazed them. There were no lions, no clowns, and no trapeze wires in this tent. Instead, laying out on the big top ground was none other than the barrel shaped airship!

Chapter 8: Sabotage!

The twins couldn't believe their eyes. The airship lay before them, its large metal frame bobbing up and down slightly, while its body was tied to the ground.

"That's how it's been kept hidden," Emma whispered to Jimmy, so no one would hear them. "I wondered how an object as big as that ship could be kept hidden. Of course, under a tent! That's why no one has seen it, and the newspapers think it is a hoax."

"Well, the coast is clear," said Jimmy. He pointed to the lower base of the airship, where the pilot sits. "That bottom part, which looks like a carriage, is called the gondola. It's where the mad bomber controls the airship. Come on! Let's get a closer look."

Jimmy took off before Emma could stop him, and she reluctantly followed. They went to the body of the airship, below the barrel frame, and they were surprised to see how much it really looked like a cross between a carriage and a boat.

"Let's go in," Jimmy said, finding the door to the device unlocked.

"Jimmy," Emma snapped in a harsh whisper. "What if someone sees us? We should wait for Sherlock Holmes to get here."

"He might not make it in time," Jimmy stated, as he walked into the gondola, and turned towards the airship's control room. "Wow! Look at this!"

The control room was much like the bridge of a ship that would sail through the ocean. There was a steering wheel at the helm, although it was at a level for someone sitting instead of someone standing. Just next to the steering wheel was a bike pedal device. The mad bomber was pedaling on it when he threw the rock into 221B Baker Street. There was another steering wheel to the side of the pedals, just above the floor.

"Why are there two steering wheels?" Emma wondered.

They control different parts of the airship," Jimmy explained. "The wheel at the front steers the ship to the left and right in the air, much like the controls of a steam ship. The side wheel is the elevator. It positions the ship to move up or down."

"That makes sense. It is more complicated than I expected. What about the pedals? Are the pedals used to power the airship?" Emma asked. "It seems like they wouldn't generate enough power."

"They don't," Jimmy explained. He showed Emma how wires from the bike pedals led down to a battery connected to the flood light. "The bike pedals are used to charge the blinding light the mad bomber uses to scare people. Remember, it made the crowd in the street scatter, and it blinded mom and dad."

"Oh, I remember," Emma said with a shake of her head. "It's not a memory I shall soon forget. But if this pedal is for the flood light, what is powering the airship?"

"Two things," Jimmy explained. "There is a gas inside the barrel above us that is most likely hydrogen. It gives the airship the lift it needs, like a balloon lifting off into the sky."

"That gives the ship the lift," Emma nodded, thinking it through. "What propels the ship?"

"If we go to the rear of the gondola, we'll find a steam engine that powers the ship," Jimmy explained. He brought Emma to the back of the gondola, where there was a separate small room. Jimmy opened the door and pointed to a large steam engine, with wires going off to the left and right of the ship. Emma looked out the windows. She saw two propellers on the side wings connected to the engine wires.

"Now, it all makes sense!" Emma said. "We need to go and stop this bomber from destroying London."

"Wait, let's look at the engine. We might be able to-"

Just then, a loud cackling laughter was heard as a man opened the door to the airship.

"Quick, we need to hide," Emma said. She saw a small closet off to the side of the engine room. Before hiding, Jimmy grabbed some of the engine wires, moved them around, and then jumped into the closet with his sister. They closed the door, just in time, as three men entered the engine room.

The twins could see the first man was the mad bomber, and Jimmy saw that he clearly was not Sherlock Holmes. The man removed his deerstalker hat, and he ruffled his hands through his scraggly gray hair. He was short and stocky, had piercing, wicked black eyes, a wrinkly forehead, and was missing a chunk of the top of his left ear. The henchmen were muscular, bald, and covered in tattoos.

"Wait until Sherlock Holmes and his brother see what I have in store for them," the mad bomber said and held up a small bundle of dynamite sticks taped together. "Now that I have the final ingredients from the apothecary, the dynamite is complete. The Holmes brothers will be at 221B Baker Street, expecting me to collect the ransom. Instead, I will toss this dynamite to them and Boom!" the bomber said and threw his arms up in the air, acting like an explosion. His two henchmen laughed.

"But boss," one of the henchmen said, "Why don't we collect the money? You had them bring a million pounds to the house."

"Moron!" the bomber yelled at the henchman. "Don't be so stupid! Once I blow up Sherlock Holmes and his brother Mycroft, then everyone will know my power. We can have as much money as we want. We can take over London. We could even take over the entire world!"

The twins gasped in horror at the mad bomber's plan.

"Now," the mad bomber continued, "It is time. Hand me my escape pack," he said to the shorter of the two henchmen, who handed the mad bomber something that looked like a backpack. "Ready the tent!" he called to them, and the two henchmen left the aircraft.

"What are we going to do?" asked Emma. "If we leave, they'll see us."

"I know," Jimmy said. "We might be able to-"

Jimmy was interrupted by the loud roar of the steam engine. The twins opened the door to the closet and peeked out. No one was in the engine room. "Quick! Let's go!" Jimmy exclaimed.

The twins got out, just to see that they were too late. Jimmy and Emma felt a shifting under their feet as the airship lifted into the air.

"Oh, No!" Emma called. She and Jimmy looked out the window. They saw the henchmen pull back the top sheets of the big top tent. The airship continued upwards and upwards into the sky, heading to London, heading to destroy Sherlock Holmes!

Chapter 9: An Amazing Escape

As the airship lifted further and further into the sky, Jimmy and Emma saw the tent below them get smaller and smaller. It felt like the ship was going to touch the sun, when suddenly, it paused in the air and began moving forward through the clouds, heading straight for London.

"We have to stop the bomber!" Emma stated. "We have to save London!"

"Don't worry about London," Jimmy said, pointing to the steam engine. "I reversed some of the wires, just give it a second and-"

BANG! Huge sparks shot out of the side of the steam engine. It sputtered and stopped working. Jimmy and Emma ran back to the closet as they heard the mad bomber approaching. Before closing the door, Emma gave Jimmy a thumbs up for destroying the engine.

"What is this?!" The mad bomber screamed as he looked at the engine. "It's ruined! I'll never be able to fix this now! But who could have…"

The mad bomber reached for the handle of the closet, and with a quick turn and a yank, he flung the door open, discovering Jimmy and Emma.

"So, brave fools are you?" he said, and he laughed at the twins. "You really think you've stopped me? You really think I can't build another airship and attack London again?"

"You're not going to build anything unless you land this airship!" Jimmy said sternly.

"Get the airship on the ground before it's too late for all of us," Emma added.

The mad bomber let out an evil cackle of laughter. "It might be too late for you, but not for me!" he sneered at Jimmy and Emma. The mad bomber pointed to the pack he wore on his back. "This is my escape route. Too bad there's only one."

The bomber ran over to the main door, threw it open, and dived out into the sky. Emma couldn't believe the man had jumped off the airship! The twins both watched the mad bomber fall faster and faster to the Earth. Then, suddenly, his backpack opened, and what looked like a large blanket emerged.

"It's a parachute!" Jimmy said. "I've heard of them, but I've never seen one in person. I'd love to see one up close."

"There won't be a chance to see one at all if we don't get off this thing," Emma snapped. "We have to get this airship on the ground, without crashing it."

"Any ideas?" Jimmy asked.

"I have one," Emma said. "If we tear some holes in the airship barrel, we can release a small amount of hydrogen. As long as it doesn't leak too fast, we should be able to get this ship safely back on the ground."

"Great idea!" Jimmy smiled. He found a knife among some of the tools in the back of the closet. *This will work perfectly*, he thought to himself and then ran to the airship door. "I'll have to climb out there," he explained, pointing to the top of the gondola. "Wish me luck!"

"Be careful," Emma said, "Make sure you hold on tight to the ladder rungs on the side of the ship. If we hit a gust of wind..."

"I know. I know," Jimmy nodded grimly. "I'll try to be as fast as possible."

Jimmy put the blade of the knife between his teeth, grabbed a ladder rung, and climbed out onto the airship. He tried not to look down, but at one point, he couldn't help it. He was miles above the ground. If he fell....he shuddered at the thought.

The boy climbed the final rung and could now feel the smooth, rigid, barrel body of the ship above him. Jimmy carefully removed the blade from between his teeth, clenched the knife in his hand, and slashed the fabric with all his might. FWISH! Came the sound of the hydrogen seeping out of the airship sack. Jimmy cut several more holes and could feel the hydrogen flowing out of the barrel.

Suddenly, the airship gave a lurch as a gust of wind smashed into it. "Whoa!" Jimmy called, and the knife fell out of his hand, smacked against the side of the gondola, then plummeted down through the clouds. Jimmy clung onto the rail as he slipped and lost his footing. He held on with all his might, his feet dangling in the air. Jimmy kicked his feet out, searching for a rail, feeling his grip slipping away. If he didn't get a foothold soon, he would fall and then...Finally, his feet found a rung, and Jimmy was able to hold himself up. He gave a loud sigh of relief and began moving back toward the door. He had to get back inside the airship, quickly. If another blast of wind hit, he might be a goner.

Taking the last few, final, ladder steps, Jimmy got back to the doorway. Emma grabbed his hand, and she pulled him back into the safety of the airship cabin.

"Are you okay?" Emma asked. "When that wind hit, I wasn't sure if you'd make it."

"Neither was I, but I'm back inside, in one piece," Jimmy gave a slight smile. "What more could I ask for? Now, we just have to wait for the hydrogen to leak out."

While the airship began its slow descent, the twins explored the airship cabin. Jimmy took notes on how the two steering wheels were used to control the ship. Emma opened all the compartments and doors, finding hidden supplies of food and water. She even found a hidden bay underneath the floor. There, Emma pulled out a strange, large, triangular shaped device.

"Emma, we have a problem!" Jimmy yelled to his sister. Emma ran over to Jimmy and saw the big problem. Directly in front of the airship was a large windmill. If they crashed into it, the airship would surely explode!

Jimmy clutched the steering wheels, trying to turn them, but he couldn't change course fast enough. "I can't stop it, Emma!"

"Don't worry, Jimmy, I found another escape route." She pointed to the folded triangular object.

"It's a glider," Jimmy grinned. "Emma, you just saved our lives!"

Within seconds, the twins were in front of the gondola doorway, strapped into the giant wing. The airship was moving closer and closer to the windmill, faster and faster it approached.

"It's now or never," Emma called. "1...2...3!" With that, the twins jumped off the ship and soared into the air.

They just made it. With a violent BOOM! The airship crashed into the windmill. Flames erupted into the sky.

"Uh-Oh!" Jimmy shouted to Emma. Some sparks had landed on the glider. Fire burst out on the left side of the wing.

"Hang on!" Emma called. She swung the glider straight at a forest of trees as the fire began to engulf the hang glider.

Chapter 10: Introducing The Baker Street Youth Detectives

Emma shivered slightly and pulled the blanket tighter around her body. She watched as the fire trucks squirted water upon the remains of the burning windmill and airship debris. *Water! Ughh!* she thought to herself.

When the twins' hang glider had caught on fire, Emma had seen a small pond in a nearby forest. With a loud SPLASH! she had crashed the glider into the pond's water and muck, saving both herself and Jimmy, but leaving them covered in mud and gunk.

Jimmy was now off with a doctor, getting his arm put in a cast. He'd broken his right arm in the fall, when it smacked against a hidden boulder, and he was now getting it set. "You be careful with that arm of yours, young man," the doctor told him. "I don't want any more accidents while you heal, certainly no flying in gliders or airships."

"Yes sir," Jimmy said weakly. His arm hurt, but he was more afraid of what his parents would say when they saw him.

Jimmy was about to find out when a row of cabs arrived at the scene. Stepping out of the cabs were several police officers, Sherlock Holmes, Dr. Watson, Mr. and Mrs. MacDougall, and a rather large man Jimmy had never set eyes on before. This large man had a cab all to himself, and Emma noted that when he got out of the cab, it seemed to lift up an extra five inches from the ground. Who was this well-dressed hefty fellow? And why was he with Sherlock Holmes and her parents?

"Emma! Jimmy!" Mrs. MacDougall called out. She gave the twins a big hug.

"Ouch!" yelped Jimmy. "Watch my arm."

"It serves you right, James!" Mrs. MacDougall scolded Jimmy, calling him by his real name. "You and your sister could have been seriously hurt. You could have died. If I had only known what you were up to, I would have locked you away!"

"If you had locked them away, Frances, then my home would be destroyed, and most of London would be burning like that windmill," explained Sherlock Holmes to Mrs. MacDougall, pointing at the flaming rubble. "It is because of your children that we have the notorious mad bomber and his henchmen in custody."

"You caught them?" Emma asked, surprised at how quickly they had moved.

"Yes," Sherlock explained. "When Steven told us everything about the tent, I dashed off with the police as fast I could. We arrived at the tent, soon after your departure, and arrested the goons who helped the bomber. Next, we continued pursuing the airship and saw the mad bomber parachute out of the gondola. We apprehended him when he landed."

"But who was he, Mr. Holmes?" Jimmy asked.

"He was none other than Sheldon Howe, a former member of British Intelligence, working on a flying device for the British government," came the answer from the heavy stranger. "Allow me to introduce myself," the man continued. "I am Mycroft Holmes, Sherlock's older brother, and I work for the British government."

"Caw! I can't believe both Holmes brothers are here," Mr. MacDougall stated in awe.

"But if Mr. Howe was working for you, then why did he attack London?" Emma asked Mycroft.

"Because he was angry at me. Sheldon wanted us to develop a fleet of his airships. He was working alongside a man by the name of Charles Davis. While Sheldon was working on airships, Charles was creating something he calls an aerial plane. In the end, we were afraid that the airships were too dangerous because of their flammable gas," Mycroft noted, pointing to what was left of the windmill's flames. "We cancelled the airship project and funded the aerial plane one instead. Sheldon was furious, and he started upon his course for revenge."

"Wait a minute!" Jimmy's eyes lit up. "The S.H. on the side of the red carriage...that stood for Sheldon Howe, not Sherlock Holmes!"

Everyone burst out laughing. "When have I ever owned a two horse carriage?" Sherlock asked the boy.

"Sorry, sir, I didn't know if the whole thing was a kind of test for us," Jimmy admitted.

"It did end up being a test, in a sense," Mycroft explained, and he took, from his coat, two shiny gold medals. "Jimmy and Emma, because of your bravery, London is safe from the mad bomber. I hereby make you honorary members of British Intelligence, and you two will henceforth be known as The Baker Street Youth Detectives."

Mycroft paused to pin the medals on the twins. "Whenever a youth is in trouble, my brother Sherlock Holmes needs an extra hand, or the Queen herself needs your assistance, you shall answer the call of duty...with your parents' permission, of course."

Jimmy and Emma winced at the last part but were surprised to see both of their parents beaming with pride. "If the Queen needs their assistance," Mrs. MacDougall assured Mycroft, "then the twins will be there."

Dr. Watson suddenly shouted, "Three cheers for the Baker Street Youth Detectives!"

While everyone cheered and applauded, Jimmy turned to Emma. "We did it, sis," he said proudly.

"We sure did," she agreed. "Now, I wonder what's next in store for The Baker Street Youth Detectives..."

The End

Special Sneak Peek
Of
The MacDougall Twins
with Sherlock Holmes

Book #2:
The Attack of the
Violet Vampire

Chapter 1: Sherlock Holmes's Special Guests

"This is so exciting," said Mrs. MacDougall. "I've never ridden in a **landau**[1] carriage before." The MacDougall family was riding in a luxury carriage to go to the theatre. Tonight was the first performance of a play based on a Sherlock Holmes case.

"I just hope the play isn't boring," said Mr. MacDougall. "Dressing in a suit! Riding in a gold plated coach! This ain't to my liking," he complained. Mr. MacDougall was a chimney

---

[1] **Fun Fact:** A landau is a type of carriage that was convertible, which means that the top could be removed, just like a convertible car today. The landau was driven by four horses. It was very expensive to own a landau, or even to ride in one. That is why it is such a treat for the Macdougall family.

sweep. He preferred wearing dirty jeans to dressing in a fancy suit.

"No need to worry, Father," said Emma MacDougall. "This is a play about Sherlock Holmes, the world's greatest detective."

"And," Jimmy, Emma's twin brother added, "it deals with a giant, killer snake!"

"Aww, that sounds good," Mr. MacDougall chuckled, "but does it have a Violet Vampire?!?"

"Oh Dad, not that again!" said the twins together. Jimmy and Emma MacDougall were ten year old twin detectives. They had solved the case of the Mysterious Airship. Now, all the children of London came to them for help. Since the airship mystery, Jimmy and Emma had been working nonstop. They helped their friend, Nolan the Newsboy, find his stolen stack of papers. They helped the pet store solve the case of the kidnapped kitten. They even helped Scotland Yard track down a missing little boy, who was really a foreign prince.

"Dad, everyone knows that there is no such thing as a vampire," Emma scolded.

Mr. MacDougall smiled at his fiery, red haired daughter. "How do you know? It's in all the papers."

Emma shook her head. There had been strange reports in East London of a bat winged monster attacking people. At first, it was one or two reports. Now, it seemed like every other day, people were reporting seeing a strange, violet colored creature with sharp teeth, and glowing red eyes.

"We'll see if someone brings us the case," laughed Jimmy. "Tonight, let's just enjoy the show."

With all of the excitement in their lives, Jimmy and Emma were looking forward to a night at the theatre. Sherlock Holmes had invited the MacDougall family as his special guests. He knew the family, especially Mrs. MacDougall, would love a grand night out.

Mrs. MacDougall jumped for joy when they received the invitation. She wore her best dress that evening, a blue silk dress. She also wore the MacDougall diamond ring. This ring had been in the MacDougall family for over

1,000 years. At one time, it was worn by the Queen of Scotland! Mrs. MacDougall rarely wore the ring. She was afraid it might get lost or stolen.

The landau carriage pulled up in front of the Adelphi theatre. The four horses whinnied, and the driver got down to open the door. Mrs. MacDougall and Emma were the first ones out of the carriage, followed by Mr. MacDougall, and then Jimmy.

"Oww," yelped Jimmy. He had bonked his head on the top of the carriage door. Jimmy was very tall for his age. He often went in disguise as an adult.

"Are you all right?" asked Mrs. MacDougall.

"Of course," answered Jimmy, rubbing the back of his head. "Now, let's go see Sherlock Holmes. I'm looking forward to a fun night."

Little did Jimmy know that far above him, on the theatre roof, a dark form, with glowing red eyes, watched the MacDougall family. The shadowy figure smiled, revealing its sharp fangs. It chuckled in a deep, scary tone. The creature unfolded its massive wings, and prepared to attack.

Special Thanks

Derrick Belanger would like to thank all of the people who offered feedback and advice while he wrote this exceptional story: Harrison and Chris Cramer; Jennifer Viers; Leigh Meinig; Karen Cohn, your advice was invaluable; Neely and Juliana Hanski; Tina and Maxine Gosselin; Beth Mason and her family; Griffon Garcon; Mike Hogan; Mark Wayne McGinnis; Stephen Seitz; Steve Emecz; Lynn Gale; Dr. Watson's Neglected Patients; The Undershaw Preservation Trust; Stepping Stones School; Century Middle School and the Adams 12 Five Star School District; Sir Arthur Conan Doyle; and, of course, the world's two biggest kids, Chuck and Claudia Davis. Without your valuable insights, I don't think I could have made this delightful adventure.

The author would also like to thank his parents, Dennis and Ellen Belanger, and grandmother, Barbara Rousseau, for their support; Brian Belanger, the best big brother he could ask for; Traci Belanger, for letting Brian out to play; Abigail Gosselin, his wife, for not minding too much the time the writing took away from family and chores; and Phoebe Belanger for patiently waiting for the second book to be dedicated to her.

Brian Belanger would like to thank: my brother Derrick for writing this book and collaborating with me on all the other stories I hope we get to tell; my wife Traci for providing a sounding board and understanding that sometimes I've just got to draw; Steve Emecz for being a publisher extraordinaire; Sir Arthur Conan Doyle for creating Sherlock Holmes and his supporting cast, and Godzilla, for proving that monsters can be heroes, too.

Author Derrick Belanger is the editor of the bestselling two volume anthology, *A Study in Terror: Sir Arthur Conan Doyle's Revolutionary Stories of Fear and the Supernatural*, which may be too scary for readers of this book. He is a middle school Language Arts teacher, and he loves young adult literature as well as anything and everything to do with Sherlock Holmes. Derrick lives in Broomfield, Colorado with his wife, Abigail Gosselin, and their two daughters, Rhea and Phoebe.

Illustrator Brian Belanger is the cover artist and a contributor to the bestselling two volume anthology *A Study in Terror: Sir Arthur Conan Doyle's Revolutionary Stories of Fear and the Supernatural*. He has always loved to draw, laugh, dance and sing, but not always when other people are around. Brian lives in Manchester, New Hampshire with his wife Traci.

You can learn more about Derrick and Brian Belanger by visiting their web site, **Belanger Books**, at: www.belangerbooks.com.

Illustrator Dedication

To Mom ---

Who gave me my lifelong love of books. See what happened?

Save Undershaw

A portion of the proceeds from the sale of this book will go to **The Undershaw Preservation Trust**. Undershaw is a former home of Sir Arthur Conan Doyle, the creator of Sherlock Holmes. It now houses the **Stepping Stones School**, a school for special needs students. The money raised from the sale of this book will help preserve the building, so you can go see the place where Sir Arthur Conan Doyle wrote, *The Hound of the Baskervilles,* the most famous Sherlock Holmes story of all time.

To learn more about Undershaw, please visit the web site at www.saveundershaw.com.

To learn more about the Stepping Stone Schools, please visit the web site at www.steppingstones.org.uk.

Also from MX Publishing

MX Publishing is the world's largest specialist Sherlock Holmes publisher, with over a hundred titles and fifty authors creating the latest in Sherlock Holmes fiction and non-fiction. From traditional short stories and novels to travel guides and quiz books, MX Publishing cater for all Holmes fans.

The collection includes leading titles such as _Benedict Cumberbatch In Transition_ and _The Norwood Author_ which won the 2011 Howlett Award (Sherlock Holmes Book of the Year).

MX Publishing also has one of the largest communities of Holmes fans on Facebook:
www.facebook.com/BooksSherlockHolmes
with regular contributions from dozens of authors.

www.mxpublishing.com